# MY MUMMY

by Roger Hargreaves

**and me**

My mummy brightens my day from the moment she wakes up.

She is like Little Miss Sunshine on a cloudy day.

My mummy can do more than one thing at a time, like magic.

And when she reads me stories, I feel like I'm really there.

My mummy is very friendly and likes to talk a lot.

But she is also very good at listening, especially to me.

My mummy is very curious and sometimes asks lots of questions.

But she is also very wise and knows lots of answers.

My mummy knows when I am hungry.

And when I am tired.

My mummy can be very silly and always makes me smile.

She gives the best hugs and knows just when they are needed.

My mummy has
a splendid sense
of style.

And she has lots of interesting things stored in mysterious boxes.

My mummy loves eating cake, just like me.

And sometimes she needs time to herself, too.

My mummy can be a bit cheeky.

But she is always kind.

My mummy is lots of fun and loves birthday parties.

She is really good at playing
games like hide-and-seek.

And my mummy is a brilliant dancer, too.

Even when things go wrong, my mummy makes me smile.

When she giggles, it makes me giggle too.

And when I make my mummy happy, she jumps for joy!

There is no one like my mummy, though sometimes I wish there were two of her.

My mummy is SO very special. My mummy loves me,
and I love my mummy.

# MY MUMMY

My mummy is most like **LITTLE MISS**..................................................

I love it when my mummy reads..........................................................

.......................................................................... to me.

My mummy makes me laugh when........................................................

.............................................................................................

She always knows when....................................................................

.............................................................................................